# INDIAN COSTUMES

**by the same author:**

**INDIAN COSTUMES**
**INDIAN SIGN LANGUAGE**

# INDIAN COSTUMES

written and illustrated by

## ROBERT HOFSINDE
(GRAY-WOLF)

**Morrow Junior Books**
New York

The author gratefully extends his thanks to Dr. Frederick Dockstader, Director of the Museum of the American Indian, in New York City, for his many courtesies and for his permission to make drawings from the museum's collection of costumes.
My thanks also to Mr. Weiss, Chief Librarian, United States Military Academy, at West Point, and to his assistant, Mr. Kerr, for permission to use the library for research.

14 15 16 17 18 19 20 21 22 23

# CONTENTS

# INDIAN DRESS

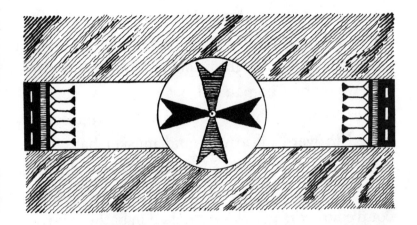

The North American Indians had three basic kinds of dress—everyday, wartime, and ceremonial. For daily use a man usually wore only a breechclout and a pair of moccasins, and in colder weather he added a pair of leggings and a robe. This clothing was without ornamentation.

War and ceremonial regalia, from headdress to moccasins, however, were highly decorated with painted designs, quill embroidery, and beadwork. The main difference between the two was that the

beadwork on the costumes of the various war society members had different color combinations.

The Indians' dress had significance to them.
Painted figures on their war shirts depicted the
outstanding deeds of the wearer. Some designs on
costumes were thought to have the power to pro-
tect warriors. The painted decorations on shields,
rather than the shields themselves, were also be-
lieved to ward off arrows and musket balls. The
war bonnet of the Plains Indians was considered a
badge of honor, since each feather represented a
coup counted (an enemy touched in battle). It was
also regarded as a medicine bundle.

Among the Ojibwa and other woodland tribes
the very fine floral-beaded costumes were reserved
for dancing, for the ceremony of the midewiwin, or
grand medicine society, and for visits from other
bands. In some tribes, and especially those in the
Southwest, only the medicine men and the dancers
performing at the rituals were dressed in elaborate
costumes.

In the nineteenth century, some of the Indians' garments were copied from the style of the white men's clothing, but were adapted to their own needs. The vest of the Plains and the woodland Indians was cut on the pattern of the cloth vest worn by white men. Made from buckskin and with beadwork added, it became strictly Indian. The well-fitted, long coat with slightly flared coattails that the Virginia gentleman wore struck the fancy of the Southern Indians, and they adopted this style.

The Indians, however, would not wear the white men's trousers. If one took a pair off a dead soldier, he made cloth leggings out of them. First he cut off the legs, put them on, and then had his woman tie them tightly to him with short buckskin thongs. The outer seams were slit open, and the raw edges were bound with colored cloth or ribbon. After a beaded or quilled strip had been added, the new garment was a copy of the skin leggings.

In turn, white trappers and, later, Army scouts adopted the buckskin garb of the Indians, which they found more durable than cloth and better suited to their rugged work. Men in contact with the tribes often had an Indian woman make these outfits. Many of them, therefore, were decorated with beadwork.

Usually the North American tribal groups developed their own characteristic way of dressing, and their costumes were as varied as the tribes themselves. Some of the most interesting and attractive are described and pictured here.

# APACHE

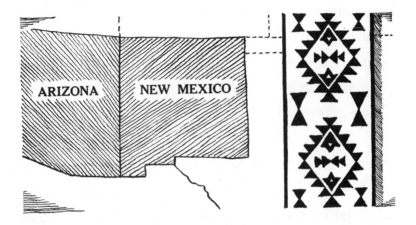

The Apache were thought to have come into the Southwest late in the fifteenth century. The tribe had three main divisions: the San Carlos, White Mountain, and Chiricahua.

When the San Carlos Apache went to war, he wore a deerskin shirt cut on the pattern of a poncho. It was made by folding a large skin in half and cutting an opening for the head in the center of the fold. The shirt draped over the shoulders, like a cape, forming wide sleeves. Along the bottom and across the chest and shoulders were tied long, thin strips of fringe. Broad red bands were painted to the left and right of the neck opening, extending vertically from the bottom of the front, over the shoulders, and down the back. Or the shirt was dyed with a native yellow ocher, and abstract, human, and animal figures were painted in fine outline on it.

The Apache warrior also wore a skin cap, completely covered with painted designs and decorated with a cluster of feathers. This headpiece and the painted shirt were thought to make a man invincible to his enemies.

His moccasins were the most distinctive feature of his costume, and their style was peculiar to this tribe. They had a very high top, reaching just below his knees, and they were held up with a tie string, or garter, over which the upper part of the moccasin folded. The rawhide sole extended beyond the toe and turned up with either a round or a triangular tip.

The costume worn for the Mountain Spirit

Dance—a religious dance performed during the puberty ceremony for Apache girls—is perhaps the best known today, because it is so often shown in photographs of the Apache. The Apache's body was painted, and he was dressed in a buckskin kilt, as well as high moccasins. On his black head covering was a fan-shaped headpiece. Streaming from his arms were two long red bands with feathers tied on them. In each hand he carried a wooden sword.

The Apache wore varied styles of headgear. One was a buckskin hood, which extended well down over the back of the neck. Notches, which were painted red, were cut into its edges. A cluster of short feathers was tied on top. Later, when it was made out of cloth, red and dark blue were favored colors.

For ceremonies, the Apache wore a rather shallow buckskin skullcap with two buckskin "ears" fastened on top. It was held in place with a chin cord, which was either painted, or decorated with beads. For daily wear, he wrapped a broad buckskin band around his head like a turban. Later

G.W.

it was replaced by a woven sash obtained from the Pueblo Indians.

The headdress of the Chiricahua was perhaps the most beautiful. It consisted of a buckskin skullcap ornamented with antelope fur, red cloth, and beads. A pair of antelope pronged horns stood upright from its sides. The wild look of this headdress was heightened by the long strands of hair decorating the back half. The hair was tied together into bunches with pieces of red cloth, which were fastened to the cap.

When beads became available, the Apache decorated many items with them. Their shirts had beaded sleeve and shoulder strips, and beads adorned the bottom of their leggings. Belt bags and pouches also were beaded, usually on a dark-blue background. The Apache bow-and-arrow cases had a solidly beaded shoulder strap, and the case itself was decorated with narrow beaded bands. Between these bands a cross design, representing the four winds, the four cardinal points, or crossed trails was painted on.

When the Apache raided white men in Texas and Mexico, much of their loot consisted of cloth garments. Except in tribal ceremonies, they soon began to replace those made from skins.

The new dress consisted of a long cotton shirt, a cloth vest, and a long cloth breechclout. A colorful calico or silk kerchief was tied around the Apache's head to hold his long, loose hair in place. A necklace, a gun belt, a belt bag, a rifle, and moccasins completed the costume.

On raids the Apache also must have obtained tin or another thin metal, for on their ceremonial costumes, bags, and awl cases they were fond of adding several rows of small metal cones. When moved about, they produced a pleasing jingle.

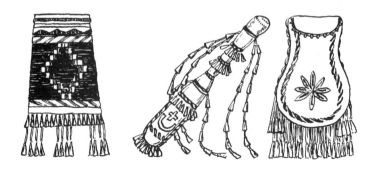

# BLACKFEET

MONTANA

This tribe had three divisions: the Siksika, the Bloods, and the Piegan. Their homes were in Montana and Canada. The women generally were very good-looking, and the men were well built and tall, many of them six feet in height. When in full tribal regalia, topped by their stand-up bonnets, they had an imposing look.

The Blackfeet war shirt, made from deer or antelope hide, often was tanned to an off-white. It had a full sleeve, which was tied together in several

places. The sides of the shirt were joined in the same manner. Long, slender fringe, or sometimes a row of white weasel skins, hung down from the sleeves.

The Blackfeet's leggings were rubbed with a yellow pigment and were painted from top to bottom with rows of horizontal stripes. Bands decorated with porcupine quills and at times quills from small feathers were added. Often the design on them matched that on the sleeve and shoulder strips of the shirt, although sometimes the colors were reversed. For example, if the background on the shirt was yellow and the prominent design blue, then the leggings had a blue background and a yellow design.

After the Blackfeet obtained the very fine Hudson's Bay blankets, which were made in England and stocked by the Hudson's Bay Company in Canada, they made leggings from them. The Blackfeet favored red blankets, although there were also blue and green blankets, with a broad stripe near each end, and a white blanket, which was trimmed with four multicolored stripes at the ends.

The most common method of decorating the leggings was first to apply beadwork to a broad strip of blue or green felt. Originally, the Blackfeet made geometric designs on these bands, but they also copied the stylized floral work of the Chippewa and the Cree. Then this decorated band was sewed to the lower part of the leggings, and the edges were finished off with a narrow beaded strip.

On the back of the leggings, just above the beadwork, a small design was added. One common pattern, said to be the head of a horse, consisted of an inverted triangle with tiny triangles placed at each upper corner. Another popular one, representing the three divisions of the people, had three long, narrow diamonds, with a horizontal bar across the middle.

In winter, a Blackfeet wore a buffalo robe with the fur left on. In warmer weather his robe was tanned on both sides. On the flesh side were

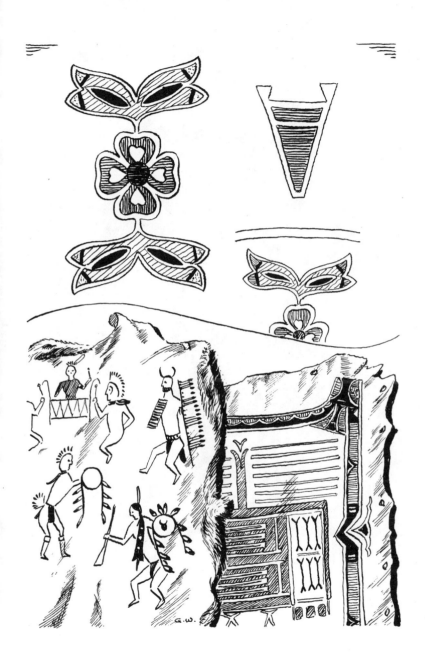

painted designs showing the man's exploits. A woman's robe had geometric designs on it, for only a man was allowed to have realistic scenes on his robe.

The headpieces of the Blackfeet were especially distinctive. Contrary to common belief, a chief wore a bonnet only on very rare occasions. Generally, great warriors donned them in battle and at ceremonies.

The Blackfeet bonnet differed from the type seen among other Plains Indians in that its crown of feathers stood upright all around. The feathers were fastened to a wide, stiff band, often stained red, which extended across the back of the head. Ermine skins and feather drops hung from temple to temple on the band.

Later the Blackfeet adopted the drooping bonnet, which was worn more often at formal affairs. The feathers were fastened onto the bonnet with a thong, which passed through loops at the base of the feathers and was inserted into slits in a buckskin skullcap. A second thong was slipped through the quills of the feathers to hold them in just the right spread and form the crown. At the front of the skullcap was a browband with a large rosette, decorated with either quillwork or bead-work, at each end. Ermine skins, feathers, or rib-bons were added to the bonnet as side drops.

A bonnet often had a trailer fastened to the back of the skullcap. Its foundation was a wide strip of buckskin or red felt. Down the center were attached eagle feathers in the same manner as de-scribed above. The thong passing through the quills was joined to the skullcap to hold the feath-ers in an upright position. When a mounted war-rior wore a bonnet with a double trailer, he let one hang down on each side of his pony.

Many braves preferred a hair ornament to a bonnet. The Blackfeet wore a single eagle feather in various ways. One was to stand it upright at the back of the head, another was to place it straight at the side of the face, the tip of the quill sticking into the braiding of the hair. Or the feather might hang from a man's right braid. If red stripes were

painted on it, the number of them indicated how often the Indian had been wounded.

Another hair ornament consisted of a fan-shaped cluster of feathers. Placed at the back of the head, they pointed downward and to the right.

A beaded headband was also worn. It passed around the back of the head, from ear to ear, and it was held in place by a narrow buckskin thong across the forehead. At the point where the bead-work was joined to the thong the band had a beaded rosette.

The various war societies were distinguished by their unusual headdresses. A member of the Horn Society wore a buckskin cap that was com-pletely covered with short pieces of ermine skins. On the sides were several full skins of the winter weasel, including its black-tipped tail. At the front of the cap, well above the brow, was a single buffalo horn, its tip pointing back. It was stained red, and strands of dyed-red horsehair and tufts of fur were fastened on it.

The headdress had a single trailer constructed

as on the ordinary bonnets. The foundation was made from buckskin and in later years from a piece of red cloth bound in yellow. The quill of each feather on the trailer was decorated on both sides with fine quillwork sewed on narrow strips of rawhide. When this headdress was worn, the Blackfeet's face was painted yellow, with a red band across the eyes and still another across the mouth.

A man in the Buffalo Bull Society wore a headdress whose cap also was covered completely with strips of ermine skins. The buffalo horn on top was split in half, making two uniform sections, so that the headdress seemed to have two horns. The pieces were painted red or wrapped in red cloth. The left half of the headdress was dyed yellow, the right half red. At ceremonies a man's face was painted to match it, the division running along the ridge of his nose. Only his lips were their natural color.

# CROW

The Crow Indians were divided into two groups, the Mountain Crows of southern Montana and northern Wyoming and the River Crows, who made their home along the Yellowstone River.

The artistry of this tribe is clearly shown by their splendid costumes. The bib on their war shirt was a characteristic feature of the Crow dress. It was rectangular and placed horizontally on the shirt, whereas most Western tribes used a triangular shape. The bib was beaded in horizontal stripes and was decorated with two whole white weasel skins at each side. Between them hung long hair locks, wrapped with red cloth where they were fastened to the bib. The shirt had wide sleeve and shoulder strips, whose edges were also trimmed with weasel skins.

The Crow's leggings were tight-fitting, and from the knee down they were stained green. The legging strip had a blue background, and its design was different from that on the shirt. Around the bottom of the leggings were two bands of beadwork, and below each of them was a short fringe.

In earlier times the Crows wore their hair hanging loosely. Their typical hairstyle consisted of braids at the sides of the head and a high pompadour on top. Some warriors stiffened their pompadour to make it stand erect.

The Crows wore two types of moccasins. One was made from a piece of skin that was folded and sewed along the outer edge. The other had soft buckskin pieces sewed to a rawhide sole. This kind

often was decorated with a narrow band of quill-work just above the sole. If the wearer had performed some heroic deed in summer, when the grass was green, his moccasins were stained green. If a man lost a relative in a battle where he himself had been wounded, his left moccasin was decorated with black quills, his right, with red quills. Wolf tails trailing from the heels of a man's moccasins indicated that he had counted coup upon an enemy.

The beadwork of the Crow Indians differed greatly from that of other tribes and was recognizable by their use of large solid designs. Light and dark blue, green, yellow, and red were the colors most commonly used. Their robes were beautifully decorated with beadwork, as well as painted or quilled designs, or a combination of all three. A man always kept his robe near at hand to put on if unexpected visitors arrived.

Among the Crows, however, beadwork was used for far more than personal adornment. Cradleboards, for instance, were given the same attention. The hood shading the child's face and the

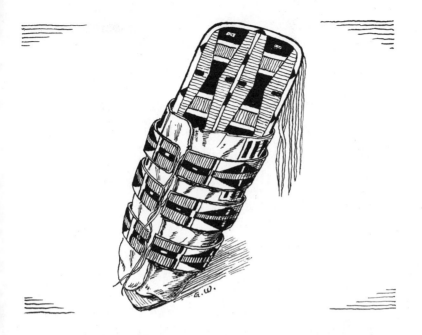

wide straps holding him securely in place were solidly beaded.

Saddles were also beautifully ornamented. From the tips of the elk horns, rising high from the front and back, hung beaded pendants. The sides of the bow-shaped stirrups were decorated with beadwork, and below the platform on which the foot rested hung a wide panel of beads and fringe.

Usually a folded section of buffalo hide tanned with the fur left on served as a saddle pad.

In many cases, it was covered with a highly beaded saddle blanket also of soft tanned buffalo skin. It was rectangular and had a wide beaded band along its edges, the two longest sides extending beyond the blanket. Double saddle bags, often draped across the horse directly behind the saddle, were adorned with broad beadwork and very long fringe.

The riding gear of the women was often decorated further with a broad band, also of beadwork, hung around the neck of the horse. The lower ends were joined together with a wide rectangular piece of beadwork, which rested across the horse's chest.

From his forelock was suspended a large beaded rosette, trimmed with bristling tufts of horsehair, alternately dyed red, yellow, and black in inch-wide sections. At the bottom of the rosette was a beaded pendant, which hung between the horse's eyes. Even the wide wrist strap on the rider's quirt was ornamented to match the rest of the trappings.

# IROQUOIS

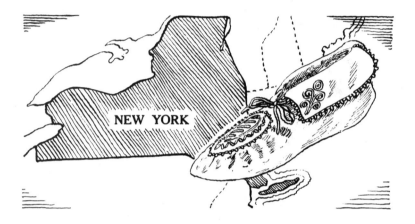

The League of the Iroquois came into being in 1570. Originally, it consisted of five tribes: the Mohawk, Oneida, Onondaga, Cayuga, and Seneca. In 1772, the Tuscarora joined the League when they were driven out of the Carolinas, and it became known as the Six Nations.

The confederacy lived in New York State. Other groups belonging to the Iroquoian language stock lived in Canada and from Chesapeake Bay

south to the Carolinas and Tennessee. The Chero-
kee were of this language family.

An Iroquois woman wore a wraparound skirt.
It overlapped at the front, enabling her to throw it
back and use her bare thigh as a work surface upon
which to roll strips of buckskin or vegetable fibers.
In winter, she also wore a robe. Later knee-high
leggings and moccasins were added to the costume.

The earliest costume of an Iroquois man was a
skin breechclout, and in cold weather he added a
bearskin fur robe. In time, he wore a head covering of a skin from a small animal, such as the raccoon, or a turban of soft skin or wool. It was decorated with trimmings of dyed hair and feathers.

He also wore necklaces made of bear claws
and belts ornamented with quillwork. A belt,
which he wound around his waist twice and tied
in front, also supported his war club and knife.

His dress leggings had an open front seam extending for about six inches from the bottom. Fine

quillwork was added, and a narrow design, also worked in quills, was placed on both sides of the seam. Over his breechclout and leggings he wore a fringed and embroidered deerskin kilt, which was an essential part of his dance costume.

A chief wore a deerskin sash, also decorated. It passed over his right shoulder, diagonally across his chest, and was tied on the left side. During ceremonials this sash was replaced with one woven of native fibers or of brightly colored yarn with long fringes. The sash was the most prized item in the chief's regalia.

Although an Iroquois generally wore his hair in long braids, a warrior shaved, or singed, most of his hair, leaving only a scalp lock. For protection in battle he donned a bowl-shaped cap made from two layers of woven willow sticks. Later this skull-cap developed into the *gustoweh*, a hat built over a light frame of split cedar strips. A circular piece fitted around the forehead, and two cross strips arching over the head were fastened to it. This foundation was covered with buckskin. The bot-

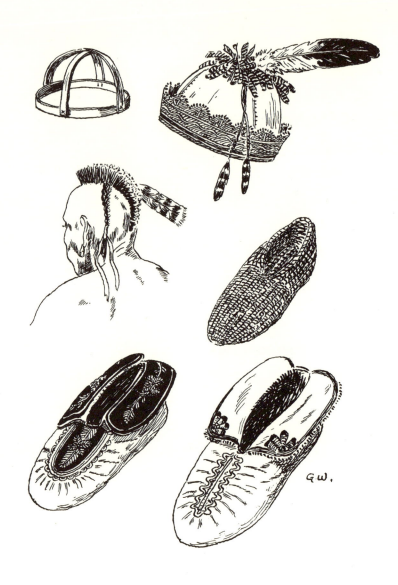

GW.

tom rim was decorated with a quilled, and later a silver, band.

On top of the cap was fastened a cluster of turkey feathers that had been stripped from their quills. In the center stood an eagle feather, leaning slightly to the back. It was set into a hollow bone socket in such a manner that the slightest breeze, or the movement of the wearer, made it twirl or quiver. On the warpath a man wore a head roach similar to that of the Ojibwa, which is described in Chapter 7.

The earliest Iroquois moccasins were made from braided corn husks or basswood fiber. Their buckskin moccasins were soft-soled. Those made by the Cayuga and Seneca had a seam up the back of the heel and one along the top of the foot. The seams were pounded to make them lie flat, so that they could be covered with a narrow band of quillwork or beadwork. The Mohawk patterned their moccasins after the style of the Algonquins. They also had a heel seam, but a U-shaped vamp.

All of the Iroquois moccasins had a cuff

around the top. On the women's it was made in one piece; on the men's it was split at the back.

The cuff and the U-shaped vamp were highly decorated. Since moccasins wore out quickly, and beadwork and quillwork were time-consuming, the women usually made the decorations on extra pieces of skin or cloth, which they sewed onto the original moccasin. Then these pieces simply were transferred to a new pair when needed.

During the colonial period the Iroquois began to wear hunting coats and trousers in the European style, but made from leather. The skins were cut into several panels to give the coat a proper fit. The shoulder and sleeve seams, the bottom, and the collar were fringed. The wide collar and the cuffs had quilled or beaded designs. The coat was closed with brass buttons.

Records show that the Iroquois were trading with the French, English, and Dutch for commercial cloth as early as 1537. Broadcloth and calico, sometimes called turkey cloth, were in general use in the seventeenth century.

A woman's skirt, reserved for dress affairs, was broadcloth, and its borders were decorated with beads, usually white, silk ribbon, or a combination of both. The most popular design was the sky-dome symbol with the tree of life growing from the top of it. She also wore a long calico tunic, with sleeves, and leggings, reaching to her knees, of red or blue cloth.

G.W.

TREE OF LIFE

A Tuscarora or Seneca woman wore a beaded cap copied from the style of the Scotch cap. Made of cloth or felt, the foundation was covered with black velvet and was beautifully ornamented with a beaded floral design.

At ceremonies a woman carried a quilled or beaded shoulder bag and, usually, a smaller belt bag, for the safekeeping of small, personal trinkets.

In the seventeenth century, the French and Dutch settlers brought silver and jeweler's tools to America. Soon thereafter brooches, rings, earrings, and other ornaments became popular among the western Iroquois. The Iroquois of New York were outstanding jewelery makers. Nearly every village had at least one silversmith.

# NAVAHO

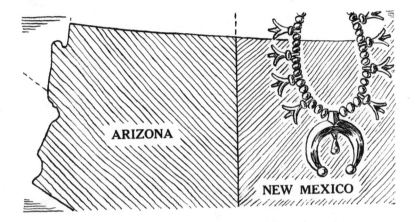

The earliest known costume of the Navaho, who were closely related to the Apache, consisted of shoulder wraps and leggings made from grass and yucca fibers. At times, strips of rabbit fur were mixed in with the weave.

After they came in contact with the Colorado Ute, they traded with them for tanned buckskins, from which they made shirts, leggings, dresses, and moccasins. Some of their clothes were stained red or yellow, but the finest of them were white.

The dress of the Navaho woman was made from two skins—one for the front and one for the back. The sides were laced together, and the excess skin was cut into fine fringe. The dress reached the woman's armpits, and it was held up by buckskin thongs over her shoulders. A cape, made of a rectangular piece of buckskin with a hole for her head cut in the center, was worn with it.

On festive days the Navaho man wore short skin leggings of a reddish-brown color. They reached from his knees to his ankles, where they fit over the top of his moccasins. The leggings were held in place below his knees with a woven band of Pueblo make, and they were closed with a row of silver buttons.

The Navaho's moccasins were stained a brick red. The sole was made from rawhide and was molded to cradle his foot. The top of the moccasin wrapped around his ankle and was fastened on the outer side of his foot with two or three silver buttons.

His skin cap was quite elaborately decorated with clusters of feathers, fringe, and strips of fur.

In the seventeenth century, clans from both the Zuñi and Acoma pueblos joined the Navaho, and their culture, including their weaving, influenced them. Men and women started to wear woollen blankets and cotton shirts, dresses, shawls, and trousers.

A man's trousers were split along the outer seam to his knees. Most of the time they were worn open, but when the ceremonial leggings, described earlier, were worn with them, they were closed snugly around his calf with a row of silver buttons.

Many Navaho men wore their hair long, tied in an hourglass shape at the nape of the neck. This style was called a *chongo,* meaning *knot of hair.* A colored kerchief was folded and wrapped around the head. Men with short hair wore this band as well. The Navaho also adopted the broad-brimmed Western hat with an uncreased crown. Black was a favorite color.

# NORTHWEST COAST INDIANS

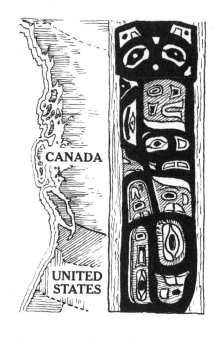

CANADA

UNITED STATES

The Northwest Coast Indians lived in the narrow strip of land between the Pacific Ocean and the Rocky Mountains extending downward from Alaska, through British Columbia in Canada, to northern California. The many tribes within this area spoke different languages, but shared the same culture. The main language groups were the Tlingit in Alaska, and the Haida, Tsimshian, and Kwakiutl in British Columbia. The Nootka, Bellacoola, Salish, and Chinook were in British Columbia and Washington, and the Karok, Yurok, and Hupa were in California.

The everyday dress of the Chilkat, who were a division of the Tlingit, consisted of buckskin trousers and moccasins, made in one piece like today's baby sleepers, and a fringed shirt with porcupine-quill embroidery.

During the rainy season a man wore a rectangular cape of cedar-bark matting and a tightly

woven basket hat, which was constructed with a wide brim and was decorated with either a woven or a painted design.

Like their well-known totem poles, the ceremonial costumes of the Northwest Coast Indians had painted designs of frogs, thunderbirds, whales, ravens, bears, and other animals found in their legends and on family crests.

The designs on the Chilkat and Tlingit shirts were woven into the woollen garment, usually in an overall pattern. After cloth became available to them through coastal traders, designs were often cut out of red flannel and sewed to a loosely fitted shirt made of cloth or a Hudson's Bay blanket.

For ceremonies, members of the high-ranking Tlingit families wore a robe, which hung loosely over the shoulders. It was made from a dark blue or red Hudson's Bay blanket, which was edged with a wide, contrasting band of broadcloth. Where the cloth met the blanket small white pearl buttons were sewed on in one or more rows. In the corners of the blanket a design depicting a clan

totem, such as the whale, was made from still more buttons. Often strips of colored cloth were added to set off the figures.

The Chilkat blanket was especially beautiful. Its lower edge dipped in the center and had long, full fringe, which was made thicker by tying in additional strands. The blanket was made of goat's wool, but the warp, or lengthwise threads, also had an inner core that was made of yellow cedarbark fiber.

Weaving was begun only after months of spinning and dying the yarn. The design was painted first in actual size on a board, and measuring sticks were used to copy it onto the blanket. The background was woven out of the natural white wool and the designs were worked out in black, blue, and yellow. The illustration shows a typical pattern.

In times of war a man wore armor for protection. A helmet made from cedar wood, with a carved and painted face designed to frighten the enemy, fit over his head. Around the warrior's

neck fitted a carved wooden collar, and wooden slats, tied together, were wrapped around his body and were held up with wide shoulder straps.

Among the Northwest Coast Indians, status was important, and, therefore, clothing was made to show off the rank of the wearer. On dress occasions a chief and other important individuals wore a carved hat, which represented the clan to which the wearer belonged and signified his rank.

# OJIBWA

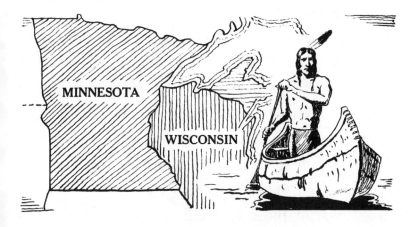

This tribe, at one time the third largest in the country, was sometimes called the Chippewa. They were located in Michigan, Minnesota, Montana, North Dakota, and Wisconsin, and they extended into Ontario, Manitoba, and the Northwest Territories in Canada.

Their earliest known costume consisted of a skin breechclout, a robe, moccasins, and leggings. Even in the cold northern winter, only the Ojibwa in the Canadian wilderness wore a shirt.

A man's leggings were tight-fitting so that he could move easily in the forest. Dress leggings were decorated around the cuff and had a wide front panel finely embroidered in moose hair.

The moccasins, including the cuff, were made from one piece of deer or moose hide. They had a seam running from toe to ankle, and one at the heel. In another type the hide was cut to cradle the foot, and a piece was added to cover the top of the foot. The sole was puckered along the seam where it was sewed to the toepiece. The cuff was sometimes part of the sole piece or sometimes added separately.

An Ojibwa woman's dress was made from two deerskins, and it had wide suspenders and a belt. With it she wore an undergarment of woven nettle fibers. Her deerskin leggings were held up with a band tied below her knees, over which the top of the leggings folded.

Broadcloth and velvet became available to the Ojibwa during the latter part of the seventeenth century, and these materials changed their

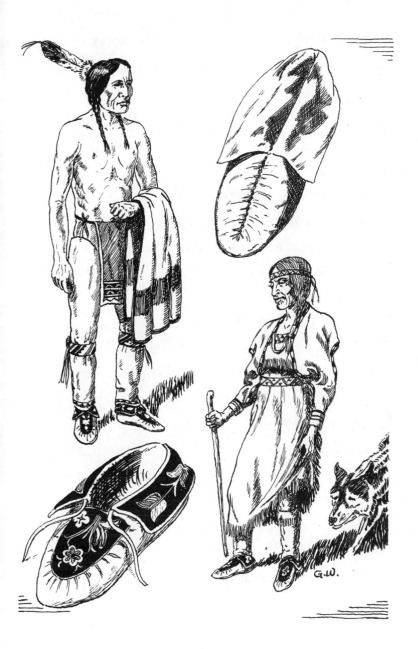

costumes greatly. Cloth garments were reserved for social and ceremonial occasions, the finest worn during the midewiwin ceremony. Red, dark blue, and black appear to have been popular colors, though dark green was seen now and then.

The new costumes were beautifully decorated with ribbon work and beadwork. The early beadwork had geometric designs and was made on a loom. The finished product then was sewed onto the garment.

The later floral designs were perhaps adapted from the appliqué work of the early French, who used patches of colored cloth. The freedom of the bead embroidery made it possible to shape realistic leaves and flowers. They were outlined first in light colors, and the other colors were added afterward. On shoulder bags, knife cases, and other personal items a white beaded background was applied later in horizontal rows. The broadcloth, velvet, and calico shirts were decorated with beaded cuffs, shoulder ornaments, and a deep bib-like front.

An Ojibwa woman's dress, made of broad-cloth or velveteen, was cut on the old deerskin pattern. In time, it was decorated with large floral designs, and sleeves were added. They were made from two pieces of cloth and were not sewed to the dress, but were held together at the top in back. The sleeve seams were joined together with a beaded cuff.

Commercial blankets, draped over the shoulder in the old way, replaced the skin robe. Their colors were red, green, sky blue, indigo blue, or white. The latter were reserved for ceremonial use. Fur traders and trappers taught the Ojibwa how to convert a blanket into a long, loose hooded coat, known as a capote. Worn only by the men and boys, it was closed with a belt, and the hood often was decorated with ribbons tied to its pointed tip.

An Ojibwa permitted his hair to grow its full length, and he wore it in braids. On the warpath a tuft of hair was braided to form a scalp lock, which was tied to stand erect on the crown of his head.

The Ojibwa wore several different kinds of headgear: a cap of burdock leaves, a turban of otter skin, and a cloth headpiece, often beautifully decorated with beaded designs, that was a combination of a hood and long mantle.

Turbans made of cloth strips and woven yarn sashes were also worn, along with one or two feathers placed at the back of the head. An eagle, or wild turkey feather tipped with dyed red horsehair or a strip of red flannel denoted great bravery.

A split feather meant that the wearer had been wounded in battle, and a red spot on the feather indicated that he had received a bullet wound.

The most outstanding head ornament was the hair roach, which has been worn by the Ojibwa for more than four hundred years. This crestlike headdress was made from moose or deer hair and the red neck hairs from the wild turkey. It was held apart with a spreader, which made the hairs stand erect. One or two bone sockets were fastened

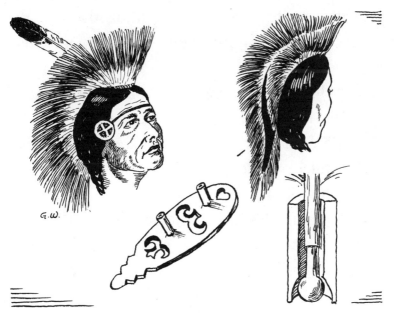

to the spreader, and feathers were set in them so that they twirled in the slightest breeze.

On occasions, the Ojibwa painted their bodies and faces. A warrior's face was painted with vermilion, and in the earliest days his forehead and cheeks were tattooed in various colors. Later the Ojibwa smeared clay over each other's backs before going to war. After it dried, they painted designs on the white background.

Members of the midewiwin society painted designs on their faces representing the four degrees of membership. A man of the first degree had a green line across his forehead and a red line below his eyes and across the bridge of his nose. One of the second degree had a green line across his eyes and a red line directly above and below. Red and black dots painted over a man's entire face showed the third degree. To indicate the fourth degree his face was painted vermilion, and he had either a green line running diagonally across from right to left or two green bands across his forehead.

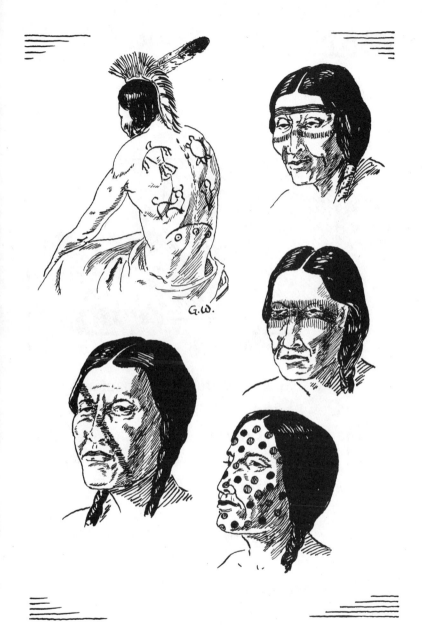

# PUEBLO

During the sixteenth century, the Spaniards came in contact with Indians in Arizona and New Mexico who lived in houses of mud and adobe. They named them *pueblos,* the Spanish word for *town.*

A Pueblo Indian wore a folded headband tied around his forehead. His long hair was braided and was gathered at the nape of his neck in a figure-eight shape. Several strands of white cord, or a narrow woven band, wrapped around the braids held them in place. At the Taos pueblo a man's hair was parted in the middle, and braids, sometimes tied with yarn, hung on each side of his face. Among the Hopi hair was often cut in a pageboy.

In all the villages the men wore cotton shirts, but in the northern New Mexican pueblos skin shirts were used for ceremonial occasions. Both types were cut on the same pattern and had sleeves. The sleeve and side seams were left open and joined together in only a few places. The skin

shirts were fringed; the cotton shirts were often highly embroidered. The design varied with the individual pueblo, and the work was done mostly by the men.

A Pueblo also wore trousers, kilts, or a breech-clout. Loose-fitting white cotton trousers were most common among the Hopi. They were split up the side a foot or so and were belted at the waist under the shirt. A knitted stocking was worn with this type. The northern people preferred a hip-high legging made of skin or colored flannel.

For ceremonies, a man wore a cotton kilt. The overlapping ends were embroidered or brocaded in wide designs. A broad sash was worn with it.

A breechclout sometimes took the place of trousers or a kilt. In northern New Mexico, it was made of flannel and was quite wide and long, nearly reaching the ground. Elsewhere, it was of white cotton and was short and narrow.

Pueblo moccasins had a hard rawhide sole and a soft buckskin top. They were usually dyed a brick red, though some were black. Others worn in

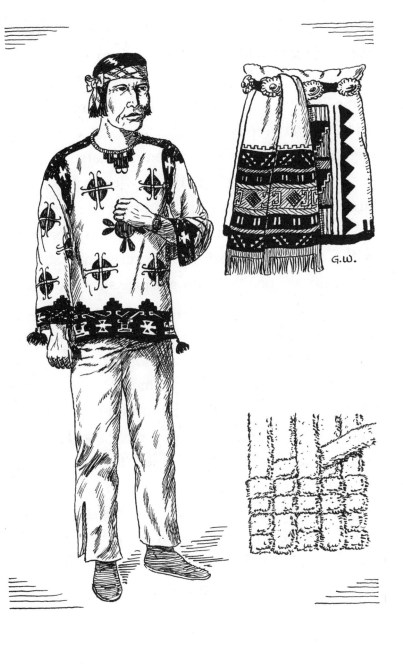

some of the Kachina dances were turquoise blue.

A robe was common among all the Pueblo Indians. The ancient robes were made from rabbit skins cut into fine strips and woven together. They were replaced later by woollen blankets.

At the Taos pueblo in New Mexico the population was divided into the Summer and the Winter people. Each group had the general supervision of the ceremonies during their respective season. The Summer people wore a white sheet covering their body and often draped over their head. The Winter people dressed themselves in a bright red flannel blanket in cold weather and in a lightweight cotton blanket in summer. Some Pueblos wrapped their blanket closely around their body, while others folded it around their waist. In warm weather the blanket was folded lengthwise and carried over one shoulder.

A Pueblo woman wore a woollen blanket, called a manta, draped around her body. It passed under her left arm and across her right shoulder, where it was fastened together. It was also joined down her right side. In addition, she wore a long, woven belt, looped around her waist several times and tied at the side, and a shoulder robe, which had two of its corners knotted across her chest. A woman wore moccasins only in bad weather.

Later a finely embroidered apron and a sleeved cotton garment under the manta, often showing below the hem, were added to the costume. Moccasins, too, became part of the daily dress and were made in two styles. Unmarried

women wore a pair with an attached spiral puttee reaching to the knee. They were made of buckskin and were colored white with a clay used for making pipes. This wraparound effect gave the wearer the appearance of having very stout legs. Married women wore a white boot, which fitted loosely above the ankle.

Rings, necklaces, buttons, earrings, and bracelets, chiefly made by the Navaho and Zuñi, adorned everyone's costume.

# SEMINOLE

FLORIDA

The Indians we know today as the Seminole came into existence only a little more than two hundred years ago. They were a mixture of Creek and other Southeastern tribes, and runaway slaves. To escape from the slavery imposed by the white settlers, the Seminole fled from Georgia and South Carolina to the Spanish territory of Florida, where they became farming people.

In the warm Southern climate they did not bother a great deal with clothing. A man simply wore a breechclout; a woman wrapped a short skirt around her middle. In cold weather a robe, and sometimes leggings, were added. Moccasins were rarely used, except for traveling.

Although the Seminole lacked a variety of clothing, they tattooed their bodies elaborately. When a boy was given his first name, a small mark, called a scratching, was made on him. When he was old enough to accompany the warriors and learn the art of warfare, he was given a second name, as well as more tattoos. Over the years more and more tattooing was done, and by the time a man reached middle age, he might well be decorated from his ears to his toes. Tattooing was discontinued when trade cloth replaced the skin clothes.

Most women wore their hair long, but the men had a number of different hairstyles. Some cut their hair short around the crown of the head and combed the rest of their long hair upward, tying it together at the top of the head. Often bird feathers or tails from animals, such as the raccoon, were

stuck in. Other men shaved or plucked their hair in different patterns, but made sure to leave a scalp lock as a challenge to their enemies.

The Seminole had contact early with the Spaniards, French, and English, and they traded with them for commercial cloth, especially calico. The women wore plain calico dresses, patterning them after those of the white women. Later they ornamented them with simple designs in appliqué.

The men wore a head covering of bright calico cloth wound around the head like a turban. Tucked in at the back were one or two ostrich feathers. They also dressed themselves in a knee-length cloth shirt, which had fancy ruffs around the shawl collar, the cuffs, and the bottom. A crescent-shaped gorget, or disc, adopted from the fifteenth-century military men in Europe, was added to the front of the shirt. Leggings or, in their place, high-topped moccasins were also worn with this garment.

The well-known, colorful patchwork costume of the Seminole came into being during the 1920's

when the Indians obtained hand-operated sewing machines. The story that it originated during the Seminole War, when the Indians were in rags and tatters, is erroneous.

The patchwork garment of a Seminole man consisted of a long shirt. It was, in effect, a sleeved blouse attached to a skirt that reached well below his knees. At times it was worn with soft, ankle-high moccasins, but the Seminole usually went about barefooted. A scarf was tied around his neck.

The patchwork dress of the women was loose-fitting and reached to the ground. With it they wore a long overblouse in the shape of a cape. They adorned themselves with many strands of bead necklaces.

These costumes are still worn by the Seminole, who are among the last of the Southeastern Indians still to follow the old traditions.

# SIOUX

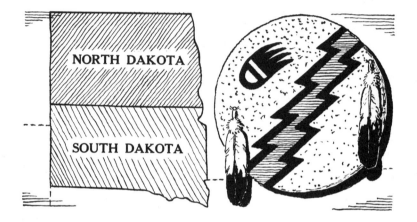

The Sioux were divided into the Eastern Dakota, Santee, Teton, and Yankton. Other tribes that belonged to the Siouan family were the Crow, Hidatsa, and the Mandan, which lived on the upper Missouri River, and the Iowa, Kansas, Omaha, Osage, Oto, and Ponca, which lived on the lower Missouri River.

The distinctive Sioux war shirt was decorated with painted designs, as well as with quills and beads. Between the bib and the shoulder bands on a typical shirt, made around 1820, were painted several guns, one above the other. On the bottom half of the shirt were depicted the owner's most outstanding war experiences. The design showed Indians on foot, a sun symbol, and flying arrows.

The sleeve and shoulder bands were of dyed yellow quills, for at this early date beads were not yet plentiful. However, these bands were edged in a narrow beaded strip in white, dark red, and blue. The bib was ornamented with a short fringe, and the sleeves also had a very fine fringe, which was long and thin, and twisted like cord.

Another type of war shirt was unusual in that the quilled strips differed in color. The one over the left shoulder was yellow; the one on the right was red. The shirt itself was painted with rows of fine lines, which were green on the left half, red on the other. Long strands of hair decorated the bib, the shoulders, and the quill strips, and, therefore, the white men called this shirt a scalp shirt. However, the locks of hair usually were donated by the man's female relatives.

A Sioux shirt of a later period used still another color scheme. The upper half was dyed dark green, the lower half yellow. The sleeves, also green, had a broad beaded cuff. The shoulder bands were quite wide and solidly beaded, and long hair locks hung along them. The bottom of the shirt was fringed.

Sioux leggings fit the leg tightly and had a long fringe along the outer seam. A beaded or quilled band ran along the fringe. The leggings were further decorated with narrow bands of quillwork running diagonally around the leg.

The Sioux ceremonial costumes for the Horse Dance, a prayer for rain, were unique. The procession included four young women dressed in buckskin dresses dyed scarlet. Their faces were painted red, and their heads were crowned with wreaths of green sage.

Directly behind them was a lone rider. His head and face were covered by a black buckskin hood, from the top of which hung a single eagle feather. Beside the hood he wore only a black breechclout. His entire body was scarlet, and black zigzag lines, representing lightning, were painted on his legs. This design was repeated along the neck of the horse and down its front legs.

He was followed by sixteen more riders riding four abreast. They also wore a black hood and breechclout, but in place of the eagle feather of their leader a pair of hornlike feathers were set upright at the front of their hood. Such feathers also topped the horses' heads.

The first four rode black horses, and the men's bodies were painted black with blue lightning symbols along their arms and legs. The neck and front legs of the horses were painted in the same manner. Next came four riders, painted white with zigzag designs in red, on white horses. The third group rode sorrel horses, and the men's bodies were red; the last group had yellow bodies and rode buckskin horses.

In this ceremony black represented the west; sorrel, the east; white, the north; and buckskin, the south.

# INDIAN DRESS TODAY

The everyday clothing that the Indians wear today is, in most instances, like that of their white neighbors. Those in the West, many of whom are ranchers or ranch hands, favor cotton shirts, blue jeans, shoes or Western boots, and broad-brimmed hats. This type of dress is also seen among the Apache of the Southwest, since they are cattlemen. The northern woodland Indians wear the traditional wool or flannel shirt and the jeans or wool pants of the woodsman. Indians in the Southeast, as well as others who work in the fields, wear the farmer's bib overalls.

The more prosperous Indians have a store-bought suit, which they wear to church, to council meetings, and, in some cases, to work. Those who have adopted the white man's clothing do not feel fully dressed unless they add a necklace or two, a silver belt, or a woven sash to the outfit.

Throughout the country, however, there are many Indians unable to afford warm clothing in winter. They are dependent on gifts of used clothing sent to the reservation by church groups or individuals.

In the Southwest the tribes still cling to their old tribal costumes, which are worn most of the time. The dress of the Navaho and Pueblo Indians —especially those in the more remote pueblos, the Hopi, and the conservative old people—has changed very little over the centuries, although some wear the white man's clothes for daily work.

The patchwork garment of the Seminole is still in daily use, but it is beginning to lose favor among the new generation.

Today one can still see Indians in their beautiful, old costumes in some parts of the country. For example, during the tourist season, at Glacier National Park in Montana, there are usually several families of Blackfeet Indians encamped in their tepees near the large summer hotels. Also many tribes hold special dances to which the public is invited, and they wear their traditional costumes for these events.

Sometimes, however, it is hard to tell one tribe from another, since the dress of all Indians has come to look like that of the Plains Indians. For example, the war bonnet, which at first was found only on the Plains, now graces the heads of Indians from north to south. As a result, the bonnet is now regarded by all as the mark of an Indian.

# INDEX

*Indicates illustrations

| DATE DUE | | | |
|---|---|---|---|
| | | | |
| | | | |
| | | | |
| | | | |
| | | | |
| | | | |
| | | | |
| | | | |
| | | | |
| | | | |
| | | | |
| | | | |
| | | | |

**2084**

970.004
H

Hofsinde,  Robert.

Indian  costumes.

**TUMALO  SCHOOL**
**19835 2ND  ST  BEND  OR   97701**

332460 01513          02678B